1

*Jack...* The light feminine whisper called through the darkness. *Help me, Jack...*

*I need you.*

Jack groaned, getting up from his warm bed despite the protests of his tired body, the urgent and fearful beckoning leading him onward.

*Help me, Jack.* It continued to beg. *Help me, please. Please, please, help me, Jack.*

The cellar was full of jars. His wife's growing obsession over canning had started innocently enough, just a few seasonal jams and sauces, but it had now grown into a tall pickled archive of vegetables and meats. It was cold in the cellar tonight, Jack could even see his breath frosting over the glasses as he made way through the stacks of rot and brine.

There, sitting on its own empty case of dust and cobwebs, was a single monarch butterfly. It was a stunning and unearthly creature and Jack let out a gasp despite himself, hesitating in slight awe before drawing near. Her wings the most brilliant pale blue Jack had ever seen and they transfixed him almost hypnotically as she fluttered around helplessly within the jar.

*Help me, Jack.* She whispered, the pale frosty vapor of his own breath hanging between them and chasing small crystalline veins of ice up her glass. *I need you.*

Jack nodded, gently gripping the jar and untwisting the top, watching awestruck and shivering as she flew forth and flitted about, finally returning to land on his trembling pale cheek with the softest of kisses.

*Thank you, Jack.* She whispered into him, letting him feel the power and soft femininity of her true form. *And now I need something else.*

"What?" Jack asked, in that moment both her eager champion and slave.

*Free me...*

2

Blood, red and slick spilled from the prostitute's stomach. She had pale saggy skin, marked from age and poor elasticity. She might even have children, waiting like stray kittens for her to come home and prepare them whatever constituted as breakfast in her strained heroin soaked mind. Jack pulled the knife out, reveling in the shocked little look in those wide painted eyes before she buckled over, clutching weakly at the escaping pool of blood.

*She* came then, beautiful blue wings gently landing amongst the crimson and burrowing deep inside. The street walker cried out, spasming and thrashing against the pavement, her head and eyes rolling back as she convulsed in the orange lit alley way.

Then the hooker stopped, and gasped into silence.

Jack glared bitterly as she crawled out from her mouth, fluttering her wings to shake off the blood of the rejected corpse before coming back to him.

The bodies continued to pile up between them as he searched yearningly for the right vessel, the proper host to once again give her form. Jack needed to save her, needed to make her whole, to make her real.

To *free* her...


...and yet.


3


"This isn't working." Jack choked, another blood soaked night ending back at home in the quiet of his room. Too quiet, his wife away on another sales convention, his spirit lover still denied form.


"Nothing works." He wept bitterly, hurling his knife at the floor like a sullen child, tears bleeding at the corners of his eyes in wet hot frustration. "So many women, not one of them worthy of holding you. Of *freeing* you."

*Hush.* She whispered, kissing at his tears in the darkness without form, turning them into frosty trails of ice. *I am patient, so must you be, Jack.*

The temperature dropped, and Jack let out a breathy, foggy gasp as his belt slowly undid itself before him, his pants dropping to the floor as he was thrown back and paralyzed to the bed, his invisible paramour now taking full control.

He slept well after his own release, slept, and dreamed of butterflies.

4

Jack was growing more and more certain his wife had been the vessel they had needed all along. He watched her daily now, buzzing about the kitchen as she grilled him about another weeks activities he had missed. Buzzing, every part of her was the buzz of an insect these days, never standing still, never slowing down long enough to be a *real* woman. She took her form for granted, the softness of her flesh and hard curves of her body wasted as she flew about him, about the world. The itch to simply force this woman still festered within him, like infected blood or puss needing to be punctured and released.

Needing to be *freed*.

Even in sleep she was restless, a terror in the bed. Their love making had been passionate, ravenous as always, full of energy that she now continued to burn tossing and turning before him as he loomed nakedly over her at the foot of the bed. The knife was a cool calm gleam in the dark, his breathing paced and ragged, his member hard and erect as he climbed onto the bed and straddled her.

Jack's wife woke in groggy disposition and quickly he smothered her mouth with a heavy hand, slicing the knife through her throat and holding her there until finally went blissfully still beneath him. He gasped, falling back on his knees and wiped the blood out of his face as he panted desperately. *She* came, gracefully slipping into the jagged tear of his wife's throat and then back out causing Jack to utter a painful howl, not of remorse but of impatience.

"No one." He roared in despair. "No one is good enough, how can these corpses not want you? Can they not see everything you would be offering them? You beauty? Your light?"

"How can they not love you?" He asked brokenly.

"*I* do."

Jack swallowed nervously.

"Take me." He breathed. "I offer myself."

"I want you." He begged, holding his head back and mouth wide.

She flew into him, a choking rush of gagging and freezing wings, then she was within him, writhing and coursing about as he convulsed and thrashed on the bed. Finally there was peace as they merged, collapsing as one beside his dead wife.

Sweat clung to his brow, and chills raked at his spine as he breathed raggedly.

"Cold." He breathed foggily into the air. "So cold."

Jack felt his own hand brush his cheek, as the other stroked his inner thigh. He moved to cover it with the hand at his cheek, and the hand at his thigh squeezed it in loving response.


*So long have I waited for a body.* She whispered silkily within him, using his own hands to navigate her new found exploration of his flesh. *I have such plans for us, Jackie-Boy.*


*But for now...* She stated huskily, his own hand finding and teasing the growing rigidness of his sex.


*Let us just work on warming you up.*

Low Bodies

1

He might have been handsome once. It was all
there, hidden beneath the sweat and residue. The gnarled
locks and thrift shop wardrobe. A ridiculous necklace hung
around his neck, some cheap tribal themed hunk of bone
jewelry that was *almost* edgy. Everything about the Almost
Man screamed almost. Almost handsome. Almost sober.
Almost cool. Almost was the extent of his existence
because anything more than that required effort and effort
was beyond the Almost Man's particular skill set.

He was, by nature, a user.

He used men, women, anyone who would give him
the means to maintain his *almost* life. He almost had
success. He almost had fame. He almost had friends.

Almost. Almost. Almost.

It was just a matter of time and circumstance really,
for his failure most certainly could not be of his own

weaving. That would require him actually lifting a hand to put in effort somewhere and as mentioned effort was not his strong suit.

Both successes and failures require a bit more than *almost*, so far the Almost Man had pretty much almost succeeded though. (As much as he had almost failed.)

"God, it is so fucking boring." The creature vacationing inside of him muttered aloud. "How do you fucking live like this? No hopes. No dreams. No fucking soul, man."

He sighed, standing up and checking his watch. The Almost Man was waiting for the 11:15 bus from Chicago. Like the loser whose body it currently inhabited the creature was also a user. It found lost human vessels and tried on their lives like shiny new threads and took a walk in them. Lately the creature had tired of the *designer* life, so much upkeep and maintenance, and had decided to take check out the more laid back options on the *vintage* rack. Slumming it. Gods help him, the centuries old wanderer was slumming it.

He knew the moment he saw her she was the one. Her smile just didn't quite meet up with her glazed over eyes as she walked the curb looking for a cigarette to bum. Her hair was wavy and unkempt but slick with oil from her lack of hygiene. Her clothes hung off of her too frail form, calling out proudly some band no one had yet to hear of and probably never would. *Heroin Chic*, he liked to call it. The wasted chemical diet, no nutrients required.

She desperately longed to be seen as edgy, but only really came off as looking desperate.

He loved desperate.

Her eyes were blue hazy strung out little things and they lingered on his for a second, sizing him up mentally for a quick fuck. He loved those eyes, a desperate twig of a thing like her could do a lot in a town like this with eyes like that.

2

The bathroom was a special sort of foul only found in the dark way-stations of the world. The creature had been to many over the years but this simply had to be one of his favorites. He just loved the overwhelming promise of the metro city depot, always shipping in a new and completely interchangeable batch of human Middle-American refugees ready for their big new start. So young and full of hope, their hearts and bladders positively filled to the very brim and *this* putrid receptacle of human filth was the first thing they lowered their drawers for. It was, poetic.

It was a warning.

Except for poor Rebecca here. Alas the first thing the hazy blue eyed Chicago girl saw was the Almost Man as she shoved him deep into the broken graffitied stall, biting on his lips and thrusting a hand down his pants, the firm length of him gripped roughly in her petite hand as he undid his belt and bent her over.

She couldn't have enjoyed it. The rough crass grunting sex they had, her faced pressed up hard against a crude drawing of two men wanking ridiculously engorged members over some equally overtly depicted girl's curly widespread snatch. It couldn't have been the anyone would want to spend their spring break let alone their last five minutes on earth but the Almost Man had absolutely no qualms in taking them from her, snapping her neck after his own swearing orgasm without even the slightest care if she had achieved her own. The creature was good at sex, but it had seemed like a bit too much unnecessary work in the moment.

The shift was simple, now that there was a suitable corpse within range he merely had to shed one skin and slide into the other.

And so *he*...

... became *she*.

3

The carnival was her favorite place in town. She would hop the fence and pick pocket the faces with her friends. Carnival friends, of course. *Almost* friends. They'd drink, and blaze, and snort, and screw, and hustle, until they only had each other left to scavenge. Then they would fight like hyenas and break up, often for weeks or even months at a time. Tonight, however, they were happy. Taking mad cash, blowing it on cheap beer, and cussing out any fucker who had the balls to give them shit. The workers naturally hated them. Everyone hated them. Hell, they hated them, but fuck them. They were the shit, and they had the selfie likes on their networks to prove it.

"Try your luck?" A female carnie called. She was tall and had a poised put together sort of cold beauty, her dark hair pulled back in a long tight braid like a little whip. Her eyes were equally dark and sharp as they took them in with a small cunning smile that didn't quite match up to her tone. "On the house, of course."

"But if we don't have anything to bet, how will you know what to pay us?" Big Bill asked, draping an arm around the Almost Woman he knew as Rebecca and drenching her in the pungent order of his unwashed pits and clothes. He slurred his words and tried to shake his long untamed locks away from his bleary eyes with drunken effort.

"You don't have anything actually of your own to bet anyway." The Dealer countered. "We know. We've been watching you."

"Sure we do." Bill laughed, shoving *Rebecca* forward. "We bet her."

"Yeah!" Came the high, drunken chorus of cat calls and assessment.

"Like fuck you do." The creature snorted.

"Come on, Becks." Bill growled under his breath. "It will be fun. Besides, you owe me for the stuff."

"Fuck off." She cried, kicking him hard in the shin as he tried to push her onto the massive steel plate before the Dealer's booth. "Dammit Bill, I said --"

Bill covered her mouth with his hand, smothering off her protests and grinning wide at the smirking carnival woman. "There. See? Our bet is placed."

"Quite." The Dealer purred, directing her hand to the large wheel beside them. "Now throw your spin, and call out if you are black or red once it has begun."

"That's it?" Bill blinked.

"That's it." She replied. The creature frowned behind Bill's palm, a growing instinct of unease overtaking her.

"What do we get if we win?" She asked as Bill released her and stepped up to the wheel.

"Something free." The Dealer said.

"All right!" The group cheered. Free stuff was their favorite stuff.

"And if we lose?" Bill laughed, his hand on the wheel, already dismissive of the outcome.

"Well then someone will have to pay the *toll* for your friend here." She smirked.

Bill laughed tossing the wheel. "So nothing to lose then!"

"Black!" He called and the Almost Woman watched the spokes tick by with an apprehension she had never known, that budding sense of unease seeping through her and taking hold in her core.

The irony that she used to be Bill was not lost on her. Would she have offered *Rebecca* up on this literal silver plate like this when she had been *him*? She thought of the way she had snapped her own future neck back in that dingy stall and knew that yes, yes she would have.

"Red." The Dealer declared with a soft unreadable grace. "The house wins."

The gang groaned and the Almost Woman felt her human heart grow faint.

"Now tell me." The carnival woman asked, looking from face to face with a probing and knowing smile. "Who will pay for this woman?"

"Sorry, Becks." Bill called turning away. "You're on your own. Wash dishes or something, we'll be at The Diner."

The others laughed, chortling their own agreements and platitudes as they took Bill's lead and left.

As they abandoned her.

"Some friends you got there, sugar." The Dealer smirked, watching them go.

"They aren't my friends." The creature whispered,

"No," The beautiful cold carnie agreed, nodding to another just out of Rebecca's disdained sight. "They aren't."

Then everything when Black, just like Bill had called.

4

The slab was cold and her restraints leather. She blinked, looking up the masked faces of robed figures looking down at her. Their robes were a dark midnight blue and their masks strange, a mix of man and beast with long protruding phallic noses and tall pointed antlers with undefined sneering gashes at the mouths.

"How now, brown cow?" The familiar purr of the Dealer called out from behind the mask of the robbed figure at her feet. Her braid was now undone, long brown lock flowing gracefully to either side of her velvet garb. "Welcome to the toll booth."

"We won't take much at first." She promised, gently fingering the glinting blade of a scalpel as she looked her up and down her scrawny naked form. "Not that it seems you have that much anyway. Just a little here and there. You know, ease you on into it."

"Wait!" The creature breathed, thinking fast. "What if I was willing to make another bet?"

"What could you possibly hope to offer in your current state?" The Dealer laughed. "Look at you! The house has already quite literally stripped you bare."

"Oh..." The Almost Woman chuckled, sizing her up with a cool glance. "You will be surprised sure enough should you win, and if even if you don't, I suspect the wager may just be enticing enough on its own."

"Go on." The Carnival Maiden offered, intrigued despite herself.

"If I can make it three days without so much as a single tear, or any cry or notion of my own weakness no matter what you all do to me, you will allow me five minutes alone with you." The creature smiled daggers at her would be prey. "*Just* you, sweetheart."

The Dealer chuckled, fingering the blade with delicate and derisive ease. "And if we *do* make you scream?"

The creature smiled with perfect calm. "Then I will show you, and only you, the very last thing I have to offer."

"Deal." The masked woman agreed, oblivious to the now utterly stacked deck as with a glint of blades and a rustle of cloaks, she and the other animals dug in.

5

The Almost woman was no stranger to torture. Sometimes it inflicted it. Sometimes it asked for it. Being human was a full, glorious, and versatile adventure of feelings and *Rebecca* could turn off and on whatever senses she chose. She could dull or heighten any experience. Hell, she could really throw them for a loop and have the universes most mind blowing orgasm right here and now as the three foot tall carnival hand to her left proudly wagged the piece of ear he had severed from her in front of her face. However, the creature behaved itself. While effort was not its strong suit it felt a sense of renewed motivation and three days later the Almost Woman awoke to a single unmasked face peering over her slab.

"Remarkable." The Dealer stated, her hair now once again tied back in its cold braid as she took in the sad yet utterly unbroken sight if her. "Alright. You win."

For the first time in three days Rebecca's face smiled.

"So." She whispered raspily. "Now that it's just the two of us tell me, do you want to see something cool?"

Bones snapped and cracked in unnatural contortion as she forced them to break and twist free from her restraints, everything snapping back into place as the Dealer gaped and the Almost Woman lunged at her, choking the life from her throat as the Dealer struggled in vein.

"Why?" She choked. "If you could have gotten out at any time."

"Because." The creature hissed, their faces now so close she could drink in the Dealer's last dying gasps. "I don't want out, I want *in*."

The Almost Woman straightened herself up, all dolled up with her tight new skin on as she tucked back an errant strand of hair that had escaped her new prefect braid in the fray.

She would have a hard time explaining her old corpse to her new friends, but they would understand and forgive her. They were her friends after all, and that was what friends did, right?

Friends. The creature had never had friends before, and what very interesting games these new friends of hers seemed to love to play.

"I always knew I loved the carnival." She smiled.

The Keeper

1

There was a shop on the corner of Market and Main. It was an old shop of mismatched brick and mortar. A relic of a different age, an age where buildings were designed and crafted by hand with a personalized touch long since lost once the cold hand of industry had traded such things away for the promise of convenience and expedition.

There was nothing precisely out of the ordinary about the shop. In fact Mary probably wouldn't have noticed it at all had she not been stopped idly at the traffic light. As it was she had a moment to observe the small stretch of Old Town before her. All around her were signs. Signs of foreclosure, signs of repossession, and signs that simply read "CLOSED" with no intention of returning to their services anytime soon. However, the shop in question bore only one sign, not even a sign for its own name. The sign said "OPEN".

Mary suddenly found herself quite curious about the shop. The young brunette couldn't help but wonder just what such an establishment could be peddling to stay above water in such a dying ghost town.

The windows of the shop were old and thick, far too cloudy to sneak a peek at its wears from her car on the street and with that simple "OPEN" sign being the shop's only outward source of information, there was simply no way for Mary to possess any hint of a guess at what the shop's proprietor might be selling. It was then that Mary noticed the light had turned green and with a decisive turn, Mary shifted gears and pulled around to park at the shop.

She had hoped to simply sneak a glance inside but now, with her pale blue eyes cupped tightly in her small hands as she pressed them to the glass, Mary found such an endeavor hopeless. Whoever had crafted this glass was clearly more interested in the panes surviving the test of time rather than allowing anyone to observe it.

*Right.* She reasoned to herself, straightening up and heading to the door. *If I want to see what's inside I'm just going to have to go in there and find out. Shouldn't take long, and I have plenty of time to get out west.*

The door dinged phonically as she crossed the threshold and Mary found the use of such an electronic tune oddly out of place in such an old and tucked away place. Of course, once inside Mary had to stash away any thoughts of just what such a shop should behave like as she couldn't for the life of her figure out just what sort of shop she had walked into.

All around her were cases of glass. Towers stacked next to towers that seemed to extend all the way to the ceiling above. It seemed an oddly high ceiling as well, far taller than Mary would have presumed possible given how small the shop had appeared from out on the street.

In each case stood a photo of some deceased person of note next to a trophy, award or some token commemorating their success. Lastly, each case contained one bizarrely defining feature.

A doll. Each case contained a creepy small perfect porcelain replica of the celebrity in the photo beside them, right down to their hair and eyes.

*Those eyes.* Mary had never witnessed dolls with eyes like those. It was as though someone had scooped them right out of their inspiration's head.

*It's like some creepy glass memorial home.* Mary breathed, suddenly wishing very much she had just stayed on the street. Every alarm bell in her head was now going off at maximum at the thought of meeting whoever might be keeping such a collection.

"Just look at their eyes." She whisper aloud, backing away slowly, able to feel the gooseflesh crawling her arms as every hair stood on end.

"Are you a fan, then?" A soft bemused voice spoke up behind her, causing Mary to jump with a gasp. It was the shop keeper; a small oily leathery man who seemed not to note her clear terror, or rather simply not care as he motioned to the green-eyed doll staring from the glass before them. "She was quite the singer in her time, and quite the looker as well. We get a lot of beautiful young singers in here, as you might imagine."

"Really?" Mary asked lightly, feigning a glance around as she privately tried to determine her best route back to the street. "Friend of yours?"

"Oh, more like a *client*." He replied airily, gently stepping between her and her designated escape path as if anticipating her plan. "That's a platinum record in there, you know. I always pick my favorite of their commendations for my collections. Sentimental that way, I suppose."

Mary coughed, trying to seem simply disinterested rather than terrified as she searched for a new exit move. "Knew them well, did you?"

"Oh yes." Replied The Keeper. "Very well, perhaps even better than they knew themselves. At the time."

Mary swallowed again, now quite certain the only way out was the door she had come in through.

*What the hell, Mary?* She thought bitterly, biting her lip in an anxious mix of fear and rage. *The universe practically painted a giant fucking "DO NOT DISTURB" sign on it, but you just had to march right on into the creepy old shop with the creepy old man.*

*Great.*

*Just fucking great.*

"So, uh." Mary stammered weakly, attempting to edge around him, now fully ready to bolt for the door the first chance she got as the roaring pulse of adrenalin and blood pumped roughly behind her ears. "Is that why you turned them all into dolls, then? To remember your friends? Great work on the eyes by the way, man. Real top notch stuff, totally life-like."

"Ah yes." He smiled widely, seemingly oblivious to her discomfort as he gazed up into those twin emerald orbs. "The eyes. That's my favorite part as well."

"You know." The Keeper stated, heading up the aisle slowly. "I knew this artist once. *Lovely* hazel eyes. Swore no matter what he tried his eyes just never quite came out right."

He smiled a small private little smile, lost in the memory. "Said he could never seem to get them *human* enough."

He smirked, stepping behind the counter knowingly as Mary blinked, trying to figure out how she'd followed him all the way back here.

*Hypnosis! He's a witch!* She thought desperately, dismissing the clearly hysterical thought. The Keeper was most certainly something though, and Mary had a terrible feeling she was just about to find out what he was really selling.

"You see, Mary." He stated darkly, his smile widening as he watched her flinch at the sound of her name. "The eyes are the window to the *soul*. Damn hard thing to capture, the human soul."

"How…" Mary trembled. "How do you know my name?"

"Mary Scoursworth." He smiled dryly, making a small winding motion with his right index finger as if rolling a private reel in his mind. "Twenty Seven years old from Fleeton Ohio. Your parents are divorced and your mom is a tiresome old bitch whom you left back in Indiana with *Bill* so you could finally drive out to the good old city of Lost Angles to become that big famous Hollywood writer you always said you were going to be."

Mary balked, taking a trembling step back. She found it distinctively unnerving and bewildering to have her who life summed up so simply and dismissively at the same time.

"Guess what, Mary?" The Keeper purred, that smile growing thinner and wider than any Mary had ever seen. "Today's your very lucky day."

2

Mary never could fully remember just what had gone down between her and The Keeper after that, or perhaps she simply didn't want to.

Whatever the psychosis of it, Mary's little stop in that small and dusty shop in that small and dusty town quickly faded into the blurry haze of dreams and fractured memories until it was nothing more than a story she sometimes let slip in latest of Hollywood hours when parties had turned to after-parties and then to *after*-after-parties.

There were so very many parties in Mary's life these days. Since the moment Mary had arrived on the scene it has seemed as though she was a new and bright shining star that everyone swore could only burn brighter and brighter with time. Mary learned quickly that despite being a writer hers was not an industry of prose but rather of people. Out here who you knew determined who you were; there was no quicker path to a throne than the favor of a king, and Mary had all the kings and queens of the West Coast on speed dial. Without even trying Mary just seemed to keep finding all the right friends in all the right places.

Of course, it never occurred to her that the best friend she had ever made, the one who had truly put her on the map was busy keeping her relevant from that small and dusty shop far away from the bright limelights of Los Angeles.

Mary's work had taken off shortly after her first party and as time went on she'd gotten a bit slow in her turnout rate but who cared, she was Mary Scoursworth, they would wait. Honestly, she had never expected to make much money out of the deal when she'd first left Ohio with her dreams of someday seeing her name in credits on the big screen but she had certainly found it. There was so darn much of it, more than Mary had ever heard of a non-legacy twenty-something being worth.

She loved it. The chic designer wardrobe, high-end and respectable of course. A classic New York look that stood out amongst her L.A. companions. It was the look of a strong brilliant writer, just like she'd always imagined. Perfectly pressed for interviews, and Mary did give so many interviews. Her pale blues constantly hungering for the glint of the spotlight and the immortalizing flash of the camera.

Mary finally had a life that mattered, and she knew it because the whole world was waiting in line with big wet tears in their eyes just to tell her as much.

3

Of all of Mary's possessions from her brave new life, her favorite even all these years later was still easily the house.

The house was beachfront property on a stretch of coastline that turned the most perfect shade of misty grey in the early morning and glinted sliver against a brilliant painted sky of pinks, fire, and crimson every sunset. The best part came just after sunset however, when every star in the sky poked out from the dark above and twinkled down mischievously above the waters.

"Sometimes I just like to sit out there all day and just let the ideas flow from me." She once told a series of interviewers in hushed private tones, as if giving each of them a very intimate exclusive which they lapped up and passed on to eager fans waiting for any small personal tidbit that would let them feel even just a bit closer to someone now so very far out of reach.

It was true though, sometimes she really did just like to sit out there, from sunrise to sunset. However, it wasn't really ideas that flowed from her in those times. No. It was memories, memories of a small and dusty shop in a small and dustier town and the deal she had made there all those forgotten years ago.

Night fell on the house as Mary watched it from the comfort of her pillowed wicker rocking chair. Idly she smiled to herself, noting the familiar shapes in the stars above with a smug sense of appreciation for how well-read she was in such things. Slowly she bored of this and did not bother to fight the lazy self-assured slumber that arose to claim her.

At first she thought she had dreamed her way back to the shop once more but no, Mary had found herself somewhere else tonight. Somewhere older and dustier. Somewhere cold, dark and lost. A decayed foul bed of pest-eaten cloth and stuffing lay beneath her, springs poking out jaggedly; a blanket of thin itchy dusty cloth barely covering her where she lay naked between it and the sacrificed and desperate mattress.

The Keeper stood at the foot of the bed, the angle drawing him out in her vision and making him seem longer and thinner and he stripped slowly before her, bile hot and wet rising at his impossibly ancient leathery deformed skin and bulbous erect sex where it stood irrationally angled and uncircumcised as if filled with more blood than any man could ever possess. Of course, Mary had long since stopped thinking of The Keeper as any sort of man, at least by human standards.

No words were spoken between them, but Mary could hear a silken voice whisper in her ear as he bent and lifted the blanket, snaking under it and spreading her legs with cold gnarled fingers, his disgusting acrid tongue tracing its sick intent within her folds and against the shrieking nub of her flesh.

*Time to collect, Mary.* It whispered in time to the invasive probing of his tongue within her. *It's time, to collect.*

Mary moaned, trying to jerk away and throwing back the blanket to fight him. The sight that greeted her however jarred her in choked despair.

There, laughing as it lapped hungrily at her sex, was *herself* staring up at her in perfect porcelain doll form, pale blue eye glinting mischievously as she lifted a tiny porcelain fist and shoved it deep inside of her.

Mary screamed, waking up with a shuddering start. Her heart pounding as sweat dripped from her freely in torrents.

"Just a dream." She breathed aloud, clutching her chest. "Just another weird and incredibly fucked up dream."

Mary sighed deeply, staring out at the ocean and watched the flow of the waves as she tried to calm herself, unable to get the sight of that doll staring up with her with her own eyes and that tiny fist.

Finally, with one final long exhale Mary got up and wrapped her cardigan tighter around her as she headed inside.

Mary's love for the house was not just a matter of location it was also about the size. Granted, it was probably far more space than she really needed but she had seen to it that each room in the house was put to good use at all times. There was the kitchen; steel, fire, and fully stocked at all times. Despite her constant social lifestyle, Mary also liked to cook from time to time and found herself heading there now to do just that. However this was more for the distraction of the act, rather than actual hunger.

Downstairs was the wine cellar and storage. On the main level was the dining room, home theater, and of course the study. The study was by far Mary's favorite, full of books and all of her various awards. Mary didn't really read much anymore, but it was important for a writer to still look the part. Plus, they really did compliment her awards. Reporters loved to conduct interviews in the study, and Mary loved it too.

Mary sighed contently, listening to her sauce simmer over the flame as she sipped a glass of cabernet. Idly she paused and unceremoniously tipped some of her glass into the pot, stirring it with a smirk. "Why not?"

She took one more swig before setting down the glass and lifting the wooden spoon to her lips. Mary blew on it tentatively before taking a small slurp.

"Not bad." She mused, giving it another slow stir and raising the cab back to her lips.

It was then that she heard it.

The rustle.

There, just outside of the kitchen door.

A sort of small *shuffling*.

*Like something moving.* She breathed horrified, going still with wide searching eyes and crawling skin. *Something very, very small...*

*Time to collect, Mary.* She heard The Keeper's silent voice echo in her mind and Mary let out a small cry, dropping the spoon into the pot with a clang.

"No." She trembled, backing toward the counter and reaching back for her butcher knife, her eyes never leaving the door frame as she pulled it out, holding it shakily between her and the distance before her and the doorway. "No. No. No. No."

A loud clanging crash came from the stove as one of the overhead pots was suddenly knocked from the rack and Mary shrieked, hearing the laughter and clanging rustle as the unseen intruder dashed away.

*The doll.* Mary breathed to herself, because that's what it was, wasn't it? Maybe not *her* doll, not yet, but it was definitely one of his and it was here for one reason.

*To collect.*

A cupboard slammed at her right with a high pitched giggle, and Mary freaked, wrenching away.

More giggling. Cupboards, boards, and pots crashed and slammed and Mary screamed fleeing the kitchen and her unseen porcelain assailants.

Mary tore down the hall, knife in hand as she peered back frantically over her shoulder towards the giggling cacophony of destruction that mocked her from her kitchen.

Suddenly she tripped, tumbling over some unseen obstruction mid run and found herself face first in front of a small male doll with a color pallet tied to his left arm and bright hazel eyes.

"No. No. No. No. *No!*" Mary cried, wrenching away and shaking off the other doll gripping her legs where she had tripped over it as she crawled desperately toward her open study door. The hazel eyed artist lunged for her, biting deep into her shoulder and Mary shrieked stabbing wildly at him with the butcher knife as she crawled for the safety of her study. The artist kicked away the blade, refusing to relinquish the painful tearing grip of his tiny porcelain teeth on her shoulder blade and Mary moaned, finally edging into the study only to feel all the color drain from her face in a pool of dread at the sight that greeted her there.

There, staring down at her with wide glinting emerald orbs was the familiar porcelain face of one tiny platinum winning songstress from the shop.

She was holding something in her hand and at first
Mary couldn't quite make it out in the darkness, but as she
felt the mob of tiny hands and feet stamping and holding
her down the doll moved closer. It was then that Mary was
able to make out the glinting shape of her Academy Award.

Then the doll brought it down, and with a sick thud
all went dark.

4

Mary came-to strung up in a dusty backroom,
dozens of eyes peering down at her from their little glass
shelves. She didn't need to see their small glinting faces
behind the glass to know where she was, the smell of dust
and age told her what she had already known. No matter
how impossible, Mary was back in the shop.

"Fame is really such an ugly thing." The Keeper drawled oily, stepping up close from behind. Mary cried out as he jerked hard on the ropes binding her wrists, checking their snugness as pins and needles lanced up and down the dead weight of her arms.

"You eternal *children*." He laughed darkly, stepping out into view bemusedly. "Once you get even just the smallest taste of it, you all start acting out. Drunk on your own self-worth. The illusion of some new found power that's really just a glass floor waiting to smash into a billion shimmering blades and bleed you dry on your way down."

"While you're up there though, dancing and jumping on the ceiling like self-righteous toddlers." He smirked gesturing at their captive porcelain audience. "You forget all about all those *little people* who helped put you there. You convince yourselves it was all *you*, no one else. All the while continuing to spend *their* hard earned money that got you there."

"And the people all go on and on about how you've *changed*." He muttered, mimicking their whining hand wringing. "But you haven't. You're just stupid enough to believe you don't need them anymore so you let the *real* you out to play, never realizing the real you is a pathetic insane sycophant that could have never bamboozled anyone out of their cash on its' own clear lack of charm."

"There's just no sincerity in the business anymore." The Keeper stated, shaking his head in mock sorrow and widening his grin as he lifted a small glinting blade from the table, playing with it amicably. "Unless you count me, of course."

The Keeper leered, moving in closer and pressing the tip of the blade beneath Mary's quivering left eye so that she could see it winking up at her just out of her sightline. Mary's heart pounded wildly in her chest as she tried to thrash the dead weight of her arms against the ropes, her eyes rolling wildly trying to escape the fate she now knew was coming but finding nowhere to run.

"You see, Mary." He murmured, wandering back over to the table and picking up a rusty headset, fiddling with the nob playfully so it was almost as though the eye clamps attached to it were blinking at her before slamming it down hard on her head and prying her eyes open wide.

"When it comes to guys like *me*." He smiled oily, lifting a gritty metallic scoop in one hand and pressing the tip of his blade up into the pool of pleading tears welling up just beneath her left sclera. "What you *see*, is exactly what you get.'

Pain tore through her, white hot and lancing, and The Keeper smiled. The mix of her screams and the laughter of a hundred tiny dolls his backing tack as he hummed along to his work.

"Oh man." Eric called, staring up at the small brunette doll with the pale blue eyes. "This is some creepy shit, what the fuck Bobby? Why did you drag us to some fucking doll store?"

"It was on the way." Bobby shrugged. "Jake told me about it and Mitch and Dirk said they wanted to take in some local culture and shit before the gig tonight."

"Not what I had in mind, dude." Dirk replied, idly lifting an information card on a familiar looking basketball replica.

"It was the only thing open." Bobby shrugged.

"Anyone else notice how nothing in here seems to have any tags?" Mitch asked suspiciously, the rest of the band glancing around and confirming Mitch's observation.

There was not a single price tag in sight.

"How do they stay open if nothing is for sale?" Bobby whispered.

"Oh." An oily voice cut in, startling the group as the turned to face the shop's keeper. "I wouldn't say '*nothing*' is for sale."

Bobby swallowed nervously, the shop owner titling his head and meeting the boy's nervous gray-blue gaze smoothly.

"My, my." The Keeper smiled pleasantly. "You do have some lovely eyes."

Pieces of Us

1

It was raining the night David got into Hartford. A
dark and dangerous drive that snaked up slick roads, over
and past the cracking snaps of falling branches. He made
the drive in silence save for the booming cacophony of the
violent thunderstorm surrounding the car. He had tried
listening to music but their song had come on. Not their
anniversary song, or their wedding song, just one of their
songs. He and Stacy had so many songs, perhaps he should
stop listening to the radio all together for a while. Now that
she was —

*Dead.*

The word itself was so flat, so final in its simplicity.

Stacy, David's wife of nine loving, trying, amazing years, was dead.

Dead, and she was never coming back.

Tears stung at the corners of his eyes, a blur the windshield wipers could not wipe away and David swore, pulling over to wait out his tears or the storm. Whichever ended first.

2

David sat by himself, staring at his cell phone a few nights later in the dim lighting of their living room. He wasn't ready for the bedroom, wasn't sure he'd ever be ready for their bedroom again. Not that either of them had been spending much time there anyway before Stacy's passing.

When Stacy had died he had ran, leaving the burial arrangements to her family. Things had been bumpy there between them at the end, and Stacy had been staying with her folks for a better part of the year. They had never had kids, it was just them, and somewhere along the line this had seemingly begun to take its toll. It had been him really, he had stopped given her what she had needed so she had started acting out. She never cheated, just yelled. They fought all the time, eventually it got to the point that Stacy had screamed in tear-streaked fury that David was clearly willing to fight over everything but her and left.

"If I'd *known*." He whispered into the silent house, tears dripping down onto the screen as he thumbed through old vacation photos of them. Even now he had kept them on his phone. "I would've made the time. I could've made time when we had time and *now*."

He killed the screen, sending it dark and staring bitterly down at his own reflection. He still had all of their numbers on there. Hers, her mothers, fathers, and sisters.

Why was he keeping them? What good could come of holding onto all of those text messages? So many fueled by anger and petty squabbles, even worse their sincere little "I love yous" that they would never have the chance to say again?

David choked, an animalistic sort of growl escaping in the act and he furiously logged into his phone, deleting all of Stacy's texts in one final swift executive decision. Then he went through her family, and her friends, and all of the contacts in his phone that were really her contacts and not his own. He might regret it he knew, but he didn't care. It was a surgery, a cleaving away of dead tissue so that the healthy tissue could begin mending and going through the motions of healing an unmendable wound.

He stopped, staring down at her contact photo. Stacy was wearing that red dress he had bought her in Maui. David couldn't do it, one look at her smiling up at him in that dress from a tiny digital square of pixelated avatar and all he could do was curl up with her still smiling his hand and sob himself to sleep on their couch.

3

Something familiar woke David up a few hours later and he winced, killing the dim but still far too bright lighting with his remote as he sat up and tried to place that sound.

"Oh." He muttered, looking down at his phone. "A text *mess–*"

The words trailed off, silent terror stealing them away from his lips.

*Stacy.*

It was a text message from Stacy.

David threw it, hurling the phone into the adjoining kitchen, his eyes full of terror and fury as it loudly vibrated a second message alert from its place on the linoleum.

"Bonnie." He whispered, Stacy's sister's name. It must be Bonnie, no way Stacy's parents would have been up at this hour.

*But there's no service on Stacy's phone.* His brain whispered treacherously, and it was right. It had been cut out last week before the month's end.

*Dead phone.* His mind whispered cruelly in that same almost foreign voice. *Dead wife.*

His cell phone lay silent now, from its shunned place in the kitchen. Cautiously, determinedly, David approached, eying the little electronic envelope with Stacy's photo and the promise of not one but *two* unopened messages waiting for him beyond the lock screen.

David had then, an almost premonition of sorts, a terrifying sixth sense that he must *never* read those messages. It was the same sort of deep primal ingrained knowledge that he had felt as a child hiding under his blankets knowing he must not poke his head out to see what was on the other side causing all of those strange sounds.

*Peer into the abyss.* His mind offered knowingly.

"Then it can peer back into you." He whispered, gently powering off his phone.

Part of him was excited, part of him wanted to turn it back on and read her words. However that deeper, more primal part, that lingering instinct from perhaps another time when man truly did battle with unseen monsters was too strong to ignore.

Worse…

*What if it's not Stacy at all?* His mind asked darkly.

Yes. That was what David was most afraid of. People just didn't go around getting text messages from dead relatives. David had always considered himself more of a man of reason than faith, but he did believe in evil.

He would change his number in the morning, he had been planning to do it soon enough anyway.

4

Oddly, it worked. David kept the phone off and bought out his contract, upgrading to that latest model he had been putting off buying (why not?) and calling up the friends he actually planned to bring with him into this new post-Stacy part of his life.

All deaths and births put things in perspective and David was ready to try and press on, in the hopes that work and time would help heal the ache of loss.

David was a professor of Sociology at the University, and part of his course was covering the mentality of social media and how it has changed, and continues to change modern society. There is a mindset of overwhelming security when one logs onto to a network. You do so from your home, comfortably, protected by not only physical distance and shelter but the crisp clean design of the network promising a neatly kempt system ever further between you and that online world. Then you have a whole slew of options from your *best* face (literally or constructed), clever names, and areas of mutual interest where you can be certain to avoid conflict as everyone there is exactly like you. However, even if you can't avoid conflict, your personal body is in no real harm. Thus, guarded by all this armor you now feel invincible to take on whatever opinion you may feel and verbally battle for it to the death. Anything from Saturday morning cartoons to basic human rights in countries you yourself will never even go on to visit. It's easy to gather a mob when marching comes without fear of physical repercussions and the assurances of thousands of like-minds.

There was another thing about social media, your profiles often stayed open after your death.

It bothered David, as he sat there at his desktop, staring at the shrine that had become his dead wife's network page. Thousands of strangers sending digital stickers, photos of flowers, and memes of inspiration. It was terrible. Tacky, fake, and terrible. David wanted to vomit, but more-so he wanted to beat himself, beat himself bloody at the fury that he hadn't the first clue what his wife's profile password was to end all of this.

A ding cut out in the study, and David looked down to see a little pop-up bubble from Stacy on the instant messager and he read it in the split second he acknowledged it without even meaning to.

**Stacy:** "MauiBirds2007"

David stared, pale, shaken, both horrified and broken by Stacy's message in the same exact moment. Of course it was, that was the last time they had been truly happy, and the last time *he* had been truly romantic.

The last…

*ding*

**Stacy:** "It's okay, I love you too."

David cried out, logging out furiously and into Stacy's account with her haunted password of promise. Of course it took and with a wet pained sob he hit delete, assuring the network that yes he was fucking sure he wanted to deactivate, before collapsing uncontrollably into his keyboard and sobbing himself off to sleep once more.

5

Morgan stared at him, his dark hands slightly paled as he clutched his mug in a light sweat. "Wow, that's some shit."

Morgan was David's longtime friend and a dean in the Science Department, David had figured Morgan would assume he was cracking up but now from the look in his friend's eyes David was even more afraid to see belief. That meant it was *real*, he had known as much, but still had been hoping for something simple. Something curable with a pill and perhaps a few sessions with Dr. Miller, not that he was actually being haunted by his dead wife.

"Yeah… you couldn't pay me to fuck with that kinda shit." Morgan finally spoke up intently. "If Sarah died and sent me a text message, photo post, whatever, you can be damn sure I'd have smashed every last piece of technology in the house."

"I've seriously considered it." David replied, taking a sip of his own coffee just to have something else to focus on.

"When you think about it though, think about all the things we leave behind?" Morgan stated, setting his own mug down on the desk. "Well if the Native Americans believed cameras steal souls then the average teenage girl must be stealing her own soul five times a day. With mirrors too, that's a two-for-one soul loss right there."

"Come on." David groaned.

"Now, imagine what they would think if they knew that not only are we storing every memory from the mundane Tuesday night out to our children's first steps not only in pictures, but even in full length moving videos. Kept out there, in the ether, long after we die for anyone to re-live." Morgan went on thoughtfully. "And not just the outer experiences, our thoughts, our emotions, we spend a third of our lives in a digital reality where we are constantly leaving pieces of ourselves. If you have to burn the things a ghost left behind while they were living to put them at peace, well… good luck with that. It's a shock any of them can find peace with so many pieces of themselves still floating around in living circulation."

David swallowed, a parched dry choked act. "So, what do I do then?"

Morgan shrugged. "I dunno, video chat her?"

6

David sat there in the dark of their bedroom, his laptop open but afraid to turn it on.

Maybe she would find peace on her own. *Maybe* this wasn't even Stacy but some data-woven digital ghoul from the Ethernet.

Maybe.


Maybe.


He didn't have to decide tonight, it wasn't like she was *going* anywhere. Or maybe she would. Maybe if he ignored her like the monstrous noises outside his blankets as a child she would actually just go away.


Maybe.


Or maybe he actually *wanted* her to stick around, online relationships weren't as passé as they once had been. Maybe this time he could actually keep the romance alive.


Maybe.

Maybe.


David sat there in the dark, his finger lingering before the door that was the on-switch to his laptop, and waited.

Tricky Treats

The party at Wade's had let out far sooner than Nelson had expected and as such it was only with a slight buzz that the young brunette swaggered on down the walkway.

It had been nostalgia, not responsibility that had convinced him to walk that night. The air was crisp and starry, and a full haunting moon lit up the suburbs before him in glowing anticipation.

*Ah, Halloween.*

A car zoomed past him loudly and he smirked, taking a long foggy breath and watching as it trailed upward towards that cool silvery glow. Nelson could hardly remember the last time he'd seen the moon this big and trying to do so only fondly brought back a near decade's worth of candy and tricks.

On his right was Old Man Perkins' place. One year the old bastard had given them granola bars instead of candy. Nelson smirked again, kicking up some grass from the lawn as he moved on down the sidewalk lost in warm recollection. They had come back later that night with a carton full of eggs from the church's food bank and added ammunition pilfered from his mother's toilet paper stash.

Nelson had one of those mothers downright obsessed with bulk membership shopping; a true and constant slave to the next great deal. His father had often ranted about it for hours, accusing her of stocking up for some delusional housemother's apocalypse.

It had taken weeks to tear all the paper from the trees and Josh's mother had forbidden him from hanging out with the rest of them for a whole week. Nelson's own might have done the same if she'd been able to notice it missing.

The next year they'd received nothing, and by the year after that the stubborn old bastard had finally kicked it. None of them ever did learn what had finally done him in.

A little further down on his left was Rachel's house. Nelson had been sweet on her a few years back, but after a few good times they'd parted ways. Regardless, he still often recalled that final prom night spent together with a fond smile.

The houses had all gone dim now in the afterhours and Nelson noted the change quietly to himself as he headed further on down the street. Not that he was worried, Wade's party may have just ended but Deborah's should probably be just about ready to start winding down. That was always Nelson's favorite part of parties anyway. The girls were always looser, and the guys just couldn't give a shit. Halloween really was a great fucking holiday.

He stopped suddenly, finding his feet had led him someplace new while he had been lost in his musing. Before him stood a large yet mostly unimpressive dwelling. Nice porch. Evenly kept lawn. Simple and elegant, really. Nelson wondered idly how he hadn't noticed it before.

Perhaps it was its pleasant simplicity, he couldn't really say for certain. The only reason he'd even noticed it tonight was that this particular house possessed one very important feature separating it from the rest.

Its lights were on.

*All* of them.

Feelings of nostalgia overwhelmed him, pleasant and yet needfully nagging at the same time. Nelson's feet began moving up the walk as if of their own accord. The lights shimmered invitingly, begging forward his approach like warm promising flame to a cold and weary moth.

The nostalgia wrapped his mind in a warm safe fog and he found himself wishing he'd thought to wear a costume tonight. A ghost or maybe even just some dark eyeliner and a leather patch. It was fucking Halloween after all, and girls loved to play dress up with you.

He grinned sheepishly, realizing even then what he was about to do. While childish, the urge was so utterly perfect and demanding he didn't even dare consider bothering to fight it.

Calmly, lost within the magic of the moment, Nelson pressed the doorbell.

The doorbell rang out into the night, an odd but sweet high-pitched tune that lured him out of his musings once more. Something about its unique complexity struck him as off for being attached to such a simple house.

It was a tell. Like late night earrings on a dressed down girl, or nice shoes on a dirtied vagrant.

The house, was lying to him.

No, that was nonsense and Nelson quickly tried to shake his head from such irritatingly dazed musing. The doorknob turned then, and as the door fell open Nelson felt all thoughts blissfully escape of their own accord.

Before him stood a woman unlike any other he'd ever seen. Her hair was darker than any he'd ever known, and it clung around her face and curves with an almost regal grace. This was accented only further by the cut of her evening gown. Deep and flushed crimson, the dress flowed to the floor; just sheer enough to hang off every hint of her curves.

This was a woman who not only knew where men stared, she welcomed it.

Nelson bemusedly noted that she was also *far* too over-dressed for eleven o' clock in the evening, but he couldn't seem to find himself minding in the slightest.

Ageless eyes bored into him with a knowing smirk.

"Aren't you a little *old* to be trick-or-treating?" She asked coyly, tilting her head and peering into him further with those knowing eyes.

Nelson grinned nervously and arched a brow meaningfully, careful not to let her see her effect on him.

"There are many different kinds of *treats*, ma'am." He replied in what he hoped was a cool tone.

She arched a brow of her own in response and he felt the bizarre sensation of those eyes laughing at him. Each one separately, as if for its own reasons.

"Indeed there are." She agreed softly her eyes going quiet. "Very well, *this* is the treat I shall offer you."

From seemingly nowhere she retrieved a silken sack, neatly tied closed with a leather thong. He stared at it mesmerized, instinctively afraid to take it from her grasp.

"What is it?" He asked suspiciously glancing up at her now quite expressionless face.

Her blank yet knowing eyes bore into his for a moment, and she smirked softly.

"Oh, let's call it a *party* favor, shall we?" She replied wanly, her smile temporarily abating his fears. Those blood red lips evoking something else entirely and he shifted unconsciously to keep his erection down.

She noted his lingering gaze and gave a throaty laugh as he took the sack from her, fumbling far more the he'd have liked.

She smiled indulgently, resting her cheek against the door frame, those eyes of her once more alight.

"Have a good night, *pretty-boy*." She smirked coyly, gently closing the door behind her.

Nelson exhaled loudly, a smug grin on his face as he headed back down the walkway.

"I love this neighborhood." He grinned, turning back to face the night once more.

Deborah's place was only three more houses down and he arrived quickly. Blonde pigtails and a playful grin met his knock, throwing open the door and peering up at him with bright blue eyes, so very different than the ones he'd just been greeted by prior.

"Hey, Deborah." He stated by way of greeting, stepping inside as she leaned against the door, holding it open for him. "Anyone still here or do I get you all to myself?"

Deborah grinned wolfishly and slammed the door, leading him further down the hall.

"You wish. That ship is so beyond sailed, it's practically sunk."

"I was just thinking I should've been a pirate for Halloween." He offered, following her into the living room and looking around.

"Why am I not surprised?" She asked with a smirk, grabbing him by the shoulder to halt his entrance.

"Hey." She stated seriously, turning him to meet her gaze. "Rachel's here tonight, so no stupid stuff, okay? Everyone knows you went out for like a week in senior year."

Nelson stared back at her and she smirked, leaning against the wall and nodding into the room, laughter and static-ridden dance punk wafting out to meet them.

"I'm just saying, she's in the other room, and she came with *Josh*." She grinned noting Nelson's twitch. "And I really don't want anything to get broken. My parents will be back tomorrow afternoon."

"Hey, what's that?" She asked, noticing the sack in Nelson's hands for the first time.

"Huh?" Nelson asked, pulling himself out of his irritation and following her gaze with a smirk.

"Oh this? It's a *treat* I got from one of your new neighbors."

"You actually went trick-or-treating?" She asked dubiously, narrowing her eyebrows with a grin.

Nelson shrugged coolly. "It was only for one house, and she was fucking hot, okay? Hotter than you, *or* Rachel."

Deborah rolled her eyes, standing back up. "You really know how to sweet talk a girl there, Nell. I can see I've got nothing to worry about between you and Josh. Let's go on in and see what Miss Bombshell weirdo got you then."

Not only were Josh and Rachel there, but Nelson spotted Steve and Mike as well. In fact it seemed to be a whole room full of his past. Some of these guys Nelson hadn't even been in the same room with since high school. Hell, even Wade had seemed to migrate here in the wake of his own dead party, although that was probably more due to the lure of Deborah herself, even despite the possessive grip he had on Sarah from his lap.

Ah, but then there was Rachel, her auburn hair glinting in the soft over-head lights, the more festive ones painting her face with a colorful hue. She was smiling, so was Josh, and Nelson couldn't help but note that some treacherous part of him still felt jealous.

"I saw that." Deborah whispered into his ear with a giggle, walking past him to flirt shamelessly with Wade while Sarah scowled up at her.

Nelson groaned inwardly and grabbed a beer off of the coffee table, plopping down on the couch next to Steve. "Hey man, where's Tiffany?"

"Passed out at Wade's" He replied with a snort, taking a swig of his own. "She's getting to be a real fucking bore, man."

"I hear that." Nelson chuckled, popping open his beer. "I won't even take girlfriends anymore. Although, at lame-ass parties like *this*."

Both men looked around dryly and confirmed that, Deborah, Rachel, and Sarah were indeed the only girls in attendance that evening.

"Yep." Steve nodded calmly, taking another swig. "And that's exactly why I keep Tiffany around."

"You guys are idiots." Deborah stated coolly, plopping down on the coffee table and grinning up at Nelson as he glared back at her. "Hey, Nelson met a hot chick tonight, didn't you, Nell?"

Nelson twitched at the pet name, but put on a showy grin all the same. "I did, and she even gave me something to remember her by."

"What'd she give ya?" Wade asked loudly, gaining Nelson an audience. He noted smugly that he had Rachel's attention as well. *Good.*

He smirked, witty retort at hand but Deborah beat him to the punch, smirking up at him coolly as if knowing exactly what he was about to say and how to best sabotage it.

"Oh!" She chimed merrily, enjoying the bitter twitch hiding in his cheek as she cut in. "It's not a trophy, it's a treat. A *trick-or-treat*, isn't that right, Nell?"

The room laughed, gravitating towards them as Wade made a follow-up crack, earning a fresh batch of chuckles. Deborah and Nelson paid them no mind however, each locked in on the other's gaze, Deborah with a knowing smirk, he with a bitter glare.

"Yes." Nelson stated carefully, smirking for effect as he turned back to meet his adoring audience, his gaze briefly falling on Rachel's with a private smile. "Although, I assure you it was a well-earned treat, and it's *not* candy."

"I bet you got something sweet to go with it though, right man?" Wade quipped and the room dissolved into laughter once more. Rachel returning his private smile from her place on Josh's lap.

"I won't deny it." He replied coolly, giving Rachel a little wink as the others chuckled. She blushed shyly, looking away and he grinned. Whether he wanted her or not he could have her, and really that was all that mattered.

Deborah pursed her lips, naturally noticing the exchange and put on a big smile reaching for the bag. "Well, let's find out what it is then. Can I open it, Nelson?"

He smirked coolly, turning back to her and narrowing his gaze as he noted the mild change in her expression but found himself unable to interpret it. "Sure, but be gentle, that's all the haul I got this year."

"Nelson wanted to be a pirate." Deborah graciously informed her guests, snatching the bag away from him as he bit back another twitch.

"Well he's already got plenty of booty!" Josh put in, earning a smack from Rachel and a loud guffaw from Wade.

Deborah smiled sweetly up at Nelson before turning her attention to the thong holding the sack closed. Gently she pulled it open, the silken sack fluttering loosely to the floor like discarded velvet skin in a soft breeze.

"Oh my." She whispered, taking in what she found there with an awed breathy gape. "It's *beautiful*."

In her hands now lay a smooth sleek orb, just slightly larger than a crystal ball but smaller than a bowling one. Its' surface was a pale rose in appearance, like some sort of polished granite or colored opal maybe.

"It must be worth a fortune." Deborah breathed, her eyes drinking in every graceful detail. It was then that she noticed the humming. A low pulsing throb barely perceptible over the pumping bass of her playlist.

It was the orb.

The orb was humming.

Then, it began to glow.

Nothing too impressive really, just a mild soft pink luminescence painting her hands in a sort of flushed blushing light, but it was glowing none-the-less.

"Are you guys seeing this?" She asked eagerly, looking up at them in delight. The answer was no, their attentions were drawn somewhere else and it wasn't hard to see why.

Sarah, had begun to dance.

Lovely and tall, the pink aura floated around her, gently highlighting her as she swayed beautifully to the hum of the orb.

Then she began to strip.

Deborah smiled floppily, idly noting that most of her guests had matched her floppy grin with ones of their own, save Sarah herself of course who remained beautifully devoid of expression as she continued her gracefully erotic dance to the orb.

Still grinning those floppy grins, Wade, Josh, and Steve stood to join her, shedding their own clothes in beat to the hum. They possessed none of Sarah's passive grace in their actions but rather an almost feral ferocity as they ripped their garments free and tossed them aside.

The trio advanced on her and she paid them no mind, her eyes closed in obvious bliss Deborah's pulse quickened, her eyes alight as she watched as Wade backhanded Sarah hard, sending her slamming her into the television.

Rachel screamed but Deborah ignored it, as did the rest of her guests much to her depraved delight.

She snuck a look at Nelson then and saw he was watching the scene as well, matching her own joyful grin with one of his own Sarah's eyes remained closed as she crashed into it, a breathy moan of pleasure rather than pain escaping her blissfully parted lips.

Wade, Josh, and Steve advanced on her coolly as she staggered back fluidly and continued to sway, seemingly oblivious to her treatment.

"*Josh?*" Rachel cried fearfully, her eyes wide as they surrounded the blissful brunette.

"Josh what are you…"

Josh turned back to her, grinning wide and showing off far more teeth than normal. The look on his face cut her off with a strangled mewling sound as she wrenched away, eyes shut tight in horror. Josh grinned wider, turning once more back to Sarah. As if on some unspoken cue, all three males punched both of their fists hard into her soft and exposed middle, her breathless pleasured cry contrasting cringingly with the sickening soft crunch the rough contact made.

Rachel screamed, her hands clutching desperately at her mouth as Sarah collapsed to the floor. A small spittle of blood dripped from the side of her blissfully smiling mouth as she fell in seemingly slow motion. First to her knees, her hair giving her far more modesty than she had given herself, and then she drooped over prostrate like a wilted flower face-first into the soft carpet.

Rachel gaped in choked horror as the blood continued to escape the girl's mouth and looked desperately around at the others in terrified disbelief.

Laughter broke out then, a sickening and terrible thing to behold and while Rachel found she could no longer find the air to scream, her eyes did what her vocal chords could not.

Deborah and Nelson met each other's gaze, still sharing that same floppy grin and she noticed that now he too was the adorning the orb's pale hue.

Nelson followed her gaze and took in the sight of the shimmering pale pink glow covering his hands. Calmly, floppy grin widening, he rose to his feet and offered her his hand.

"Join me." He commanded, his voice echoing with the authority of all in the room. Only Rachel's voice remained absent from his chilling directive.

"*Nelson*!" Rachel cried in dismay as Deborah accepted his hand and allowed him to pull her to her feet. The grin on her face now dripped hungrily with lust, and something *else*.

Something that was beyond her knowledge to recognize. Something old. Something *powerful*.

Eden.


Ambrosia.


Mistletoe.


Still beating hearts.


Dripping.


Red.


Forbidden fruits.


Aphrodisiacs of the gods.

*Halloween.*

It coursed through her veins like fire and ice as she threw Nelson down hard against the coffee table, enjoying the sick sound of the crackling glass as he hit.

His smile was identical to her own and he lashed back out at her, grabbing onto her wrists and pulling her down into him.

Rachel's eyes widened at the sight and she looked around at the others desperately hoping that someone, *anyone*, was still sane. However, the rest of the men now shared Deborah's hungry look and worse, they now shared the orb's glow as well.

A small terrified whimper escaped her trembling lips and as she tried weakly to rise and flee only to be grabbed from behind, a pair of strong arms restraining her by her shoulders.

She peered back to view her captor and realized in horror that it was Josh.

"But, *why?*" She whispered, the terror of utter confusion weeping out of her in hot liquid drops as her eyes searched his face desperately for any sign of the man she knew.

He grinned wildly, forcing her to her knees and she cried out, pain lancing through her as the rough hard shards of the shattered table tore into her flesh.

"We must have a sacrifice." Wade murmured, his voice coursing fully with the authority of the others.

Deborah pulled loose Nelson's belt and hurled it at Wade's feet, neither ritual breaking pause as he picked it up while Nelson viciously liberated Deborah's pig-tails from their twin bondage.

"Deb... Deborah..." Rachel pleaded weakly as Wade knelt beside her, yanking back hard on her auburn hair and snapping her head back to expose the bare flesh of her neck "*Please...*"

Deborah met her gaze at this, but the wild look Rachel found there told her that she would be no aid to her.

Deborah groaned as Nelson flipped her, shattering the glass on the table further and she cried out as the hard shards ripped up her back and thighs.

A large shard of glass flew from the coffee table landing at Steve's feet and he grinned floppily picking it up with a free hand, the other casually gripping a beer.

Wade matched his grin, slipping the belt around Rachel's neck and tightening it. Rachel screamed in terror, tears flowing down her cheeks freely now as she tried desperately to fight against the hold of her mad captors.

"*Please!*" She tried to gasp again, only to have the belt choke off the wind from the remainder of her cries.

Her breathless gasping final pleas were met only by Deborah and Nelson's animalistic snarls, and Josh raised the shard of glass high in time. Blood dripped down from where it tore into his own hand like some maddened Aztec priest and he gripped it tightly, preparing to strike down through the soft flesh just above her heart.

The room glowed pale pink and Josh slammed the shard into her, cries of pain and ecstasy echoing around the room as dual penetrations were made on unspoken cue.

"*Wow...*" Deborah breathed, opening her eyes and looking around the room. The images had all faded away, the only glow now coming from the orb within her grasp. "You guys gotta try this!"

She grinned wide, showing off far more teeth than any human being still living ever should and Sarah let out a bloodcurdling scream, burying her face into Wade's chest.

Deborah looked around at the rest of their horrified faces before locking that grotesquely grinning gaze onto Nelson's.

"What?" She asked.

*She doesn't know. Oh fucking God, she doesn't fucking know!* Nelson realized in horror, unable to peel his gaze from her own horrendously oblivious one.

Maybe it had been that weird pink glow, maybe it was some sort of fucked up dark magic or weird government alien radiation. Nelson didn't know.

What Nelson did know is whatever it was, it had melted Deborah's skin clean off.

Deborah fell back then; the blonde wig-like remains of her scalp muting what should have been a sharp crack into a slick, sickening wet thud. The orb rolled free from her white bony grip that was poking through the wet red flesh and tendons that had once been her fingertips. It landed at Nelson's feet with a slight bump, leaving a small wet clump of blood and sinew on his sneakers. Nelson felt the bile rise up wet and hot from within him as the partially digested remains of the night's beers and processed treats spilled out before him.

Behind him he could hear screaming. Rachel rushed past him, grabbing for Deborah's pulse and trying to keep the blood in, but both actions were slick and horrifyingly impossible to accomplish under the circumstances.

"Oh Jesus! Deborah!" She screamed, her grip sinking into the tendons and sinew of Deborah's wrist with a wet sick shifting sound that made Nelson's stomach find new fluids to expel as he saw the raw bones beneath.

*Radius and ulna.* He thought maddeningly as he tried and failed to choke back the wet hot chunks flowing from him in painful mad bursts.

They'd been making a full chart on them last week. If this had happened the week before he'd never have remembered, now he was certain he'd never be able to forget.

Sarah had dissolved into a full wave of pleading prayers and Wade was holding her out before him like some divine talisman as he ushered them from the house.

"Call 911!" Rachel screamed in horrified disbelief as everyone took Wade and Sarah's cue to escape save Josh, who was fumbling awkwardly with his phone while Nelson wiped at his mouth, unable to take his eyes from Deborah's melted grinning face.

"What the fuck was that thing, Nelson?!" Rachel demanded, tears streaming down her face as she rocked Deborah's corpse back and forth in her arms.

*Corpse?*

Yes, she was most definitely dead now.

There was so much blood.

He looked down at the orb. He was certain he had gotten some of his puke on it but now he saw none. Even Deborah's blood stains seemed to have disappeared. It seemed so innocent now without them.

Harmless.

Almost beautiful, really.

Thing must be worth a fucking fortune. It was beginning to glow again. Deborah had only touched it for a second before it stole her skin. Nelson wondered idly where it went, her skin. Maybe the thing ate it, or maybe it was some sort of portal or something.

*Or maybe it was just a safety measure...*

A soft voice within him whispered invitingly.

*A little... trick, if you will...*

Yes, that was it, wasn't it? After all, the woman in the house had given it to *him*, not Deborah. Of course someone like *Deborah* would have gotten a trick instead of a treat.

However, maybe if Nelson touched it, things would be different.

Maybe if Nelson touched it, it really *would* be a treat.

*Yes...* He thought, bending down and reaching for the orb as it glowed up at him invitingly.

*Maybe...*

"Maybe it'll be *nice...*"

Stag Party


1

It was the steady blaring cry of the horn that woke Dalton from the grips of unconsciousness. Pain sparked in his vision and the swirling illusions of light prickled and danced behind his eyes.


"Ow." He grunted aloud, gripping the left side of his head in bitter self-irritation. It was bleeding where it had struck the wheel. Fantastic.


Dalton had no excuse for it. As per usual this accident was the result of his own stubbornness. He knew he was in no condition to be driving when he had left Vegas but had possessed the cocky self-certainty to drive off into the desert regardless. At the time the distance had seemed so much shorter, the promise of his own warm bed just a little bit further down the road.

It had been such a long trip, and he had been taking it alone. Getting behind the wheel had seemed logical.

No. That was a lie. It had been what he had wanted and so in his tired haze Dalton had chosen to disregard any other logic contrary.

Now a different haze threatened to lure and overtake him with its woozy painful pull and so he forced himself from the car, stumbling down the highway as dawn peaked crimson over the tar path before him.

2

It seemed as if he had been walking forever and while the bleeding from his head had ceased the pain had not. He needed to stop. Somewhere. Anywhere.

Ahead something twinkled in the growing light of daybreak and Dalton winced, cupping a hand over his eyes to try and make it out.

"Too far." He murmured staggering forward until he made out the shape of the emergency call box. With a delighted cry Dalton shambled on faster, grabbing up the receiver in jubilation.

"Hello handsome." A silky voice spoke up from the other end. "You look lost."

Dalton paused but resisted the urge to look around, there was probably a camera in the call box or something. Although this lonesome stretch of road hardly seemed the sort worth monitoring.

"To your left is a dirt road." The woman went on. "Take it for five miles and you will come to the Acheron."

"Five miles?" Dalton echoed, looking across the horizon in pained disbelief.

"It is nearly sixty miles to the next town." The voice assured him. "However the Acheron has many rooms and is always booking new guests."

Dalton frowned, biting at his bruised lip. "What sort of rates are we talking?"

The line went dead in his ear and Dalton shrugged hanging it up. Fair enough. He deserved that.

"Five miles." He repeated with a low whistle, glaring out at the climbing sun before setting himself to it.

3

The Acheron shimmered and danced in the liquid wet illusion of the desert heat and Dalton collapsed before it, all thoughts and movements failing him as his head hit the hard crash of sandy ground.

He was aware of the scab on his scalp tearing and the feel of blood once again dripping down his cheek. He could hear it hit sand despite the roar of pain and dehydration behind his ears. Dalton could hear something else as well. Hoof beats.

"Bring him inside." The voice of the woman on the phone ordered the unseen others. "Put him in the Red Suite."

Hands were lifting him then and the pull of darkness became too strong to resist as Dalton tumbled down into the inky embrace of unconsciousness.

4

His face was cool. Drenched in the calm waters while the voices sang and bid him to chase them down the river of his dreams.

*The Queen of the Dead ate six seeds...*

Lips stained red. Dancing girls sharing fruits and spinning around a woman in white while snow fell. The woman was tall with long antlers and a hungry look as the girls giggled around her in their posy ring.

*Come to the garden, Persephone...*

Night fell. The dream dimmed in apprehension, the girls falling back in solemn appraisal.

*Upon the altar her lost soul bleeds...*

Roughly they forced the deer woman down to the altar, one of her handmaidens producing a wicked stone knife.

*Come to the garden, Persephone...*

Hacking. Carving. The priestess ripped into the screaming stag's chest and pulled free her heart, biting deep into it and sharing it with the others.

*Lay her down in the willows and reeds...*

They drug her back to the river, discarding her wasted form and letting it drift away.

*Come to the garden, Persephone...*

They met his gaze as one then. Emotionless. Comprehending. Determining his own comprehension.

*Come to the garden and dance with me...*

"You must not eat the fruit of the dead." The priestess cried, grabbing him roughly, her hands and lips still drenched in blood as she shoved him hard back into the river.

He passed through it coldly, awakening in his room with a start.

*You must not eat the fruit of the dead...*

The warning lingered. A whisper in the silence and Dalton swallowed, wincing in the candle light as he tried to take in the room around him. The wallpaper was gilded and ornate. Gold patterns on a deep red backing. There was a fireplace painted gold to match and fire danced warmly in its hearth. The carpets were plush and red to match the walls. The blankets were warm velvet over silk sheets, all in that same blood red. Little golden stags were inlayed in the rich mahogany door and Dalton pulled it open with an apprehensive inhale.

The hallway was long and immaculate. Here also did the golden print snake elegantly along the walls only here the carpets and walls were crisp and pristine.

Snow. They were white as snow. How could anything so trampled be so pure and untainted?

There, pale and naked stood the woman of his exhausted dreams. One look at her, those long scarlet locks and the way she parted both them and her lips coyly to put the full form of her on confident predatory display was enough to assure him that this had been the voice which had led him there.

"Hello handsome." She smirked, accurately following his wandering eyes and thoughts. "Welcome to the Acheron."

She came to him, taking his hand and leading him back to the Red Suite. The air was thick with heat and scents and he tried to shake his head clear as she pushed him onto the bed. The shadows painted their story behind her as she climbed atop him and liberated him of his belt.

Antlers that weren't there cast their shadow behind her, arching and swaying with her pleasure as she rode him in vigorous ecstasy. Everything danced above him in a haze of illusion and reality.

*The Queen of the Dead ate six seeds...*

Men were joining them. Six stood tall and proud around the deer woman in the foliage. She knelt, taking the first in her mouth as he groaned and clutched at her antlers.

*Come to the garden, Persephone...*

Dalton groaned as well, his hands finding her thighs and edging her on.

*On the altar her lost soul bleeds...*

Dalton flipped her around in bed, laying her across the altar and taking her wildly from behind. The shadow of her antlers growing longer on the wall.

*Come to the garden, Persephone...*

She moaned, sliding out from under him and pushing him backward with a firm foot to the chest as she spread herself before him.

*Lay her down by the willows and reeds...*

He spread her thighs, kissing his way down from her throat to the wet promise of her ginger curls below. She writhed and cried out under the thrall of his tongue and too lost too late he heard the voices call once more.

*You must not eat the fruit of the dead...*

5

She had a throne she sat upon just to look down at them. There were so many of them. Handsome men in handsome suits. They weren't real to her. Sure she cared about them in her way, her grand bastille of lovers, but they were just toys. Distractions in her collection of beautiful things that adorned the Acheron. Figurines to enjoy, their needs were inconsequential. She owned them, bodies and soul.

Dalton wanted out. He had enough of the pomp and pageantry and was tired of being a toy. He might be a prisoner here, but he was no mere bedroom prop. He had a will, and he would find a way.

"You don't think we haven't tried to leave?" The eldest, Edgar replied. He was perhaps the creature's favorite lover, if merely out of sentiment for their long history. He was also the conductor of her nightly waltzes at the Masque. Everyone seemed to eventually find their place here, to submit to their little roles and accept her as their irrefutable ruler. "To trick her? To kill her? No matter how much we outnumber her she is simply above us in all ways."

"I refuse to accept that." Dalton frowned. "The must be a way to end this nightmare. Some weakness to exploit. Some advantage I can take."

"Do you know what the Acheron is, Master Dalton?" Edgar asked with bitter appraisal. "It is the river of woe one crosses on their journey to the Underworld."

"She feeds on us." Edgar laughed. "We are the scraps at the Diamond Gate keeping that bitch from crossing over."

Meals were at noon, four, and eight. Dancing was at ten, and cake at midnight. Their warden would trade out her companion of the night depending on her needs and whims leaving the cycle to reset itself the next day.

"Where is Dalton?" She asked, frowning out at her masculine courtiers. "Everyone knows dancing is mandatory, how will I choose the best among you if you are not all here and present?"

Someone grunted in the back, falling prostrate in a pool of his own blood as Dalton tossed aside his heart and cleaned the blood from a golden dagger.

"Here, My Lady." He called, removing a ruby mask with a matching silk gloved hand. He peered coldly into her large doe eyes before roughly slamming his blade into the next suitor in his path.

"Edgar! Klaus!" She screamed. "Everyone stop him! Stop him now!"

One by one he cut them down in calm execution.

"What are you doing?" Edgar pleaded up at him.

"Severing her power source." Dalton replied tonelessly, before taking the conductor's heart as well.

"Dance is over." Dalton called, climbing the steps to meet her. "Time to face the music."

She laughed softly, a little tear running down her cheek, her true form now slipping out with no juice left to power her glamor. Long horns, little hooves, sad eyes and skin.

"I really thought I'd be able to dance forever." She whispered. "I never really wanted more."

"I do." Dalton said, and drove the blade into her, carving out her heart and lifting it up to his lips.

*You must not eat the fruit of the dead...*

"Fuck it." He muttered, and bit in.

7

*Not a lot is known about the elusive Dalton McAvoy, or how he acquired ownership of his first and most profitable hotel the luxurious Acheron on what he called a lucky trip to Vegas, only that it was to be the first of his many successful business endeavors he would go on to capitalize on in his public lifetime. As for his personal life his only known hobby is a fondness for hunting, it is even rumored the antlers hanging in the Acheron lobby are from his own private collection of kills.*

**- Excerpt from the Seasonal Observer**
**- December 21st, 2014**

25073507R10071

Made in the USA
San Bernardino, CA
17 October 2015